PELICAN'S CATCH

SMITHSONIAN OCEANIC COLLECTION

To my family, the treasures of my life—J.H.

To Bruce and Vicki with affection—B.D. and D.B.

Book copyright © 2004 Trudy Corporation
and the Smithsonian Institution, Washington, DC 20560.

Published by Soundprints, an imprint of Trudy Corporation, Norwalk, Connecticut.

Book design: Shields & Partners, Westport, CT
Book layout: Jennifer Kinon
Editor: Laura Gates Galvin
Editorial assistance: Brian E. Giblin

First Edition 2004
10 9 8 7 6 5 4
Printed in Indonesia

Acknowledgments:
Our very special thanks to Dr. Gary R. Graves of the Division of Vertebrate Zoology at
the Smithsonian Institution's National Museum of Natural History for his curatorial review.
Soundprints would like to thank Ellen Nanney and Katie Mann at the Smithsonian
Institution's Office of Product Development and Licensing for their help in the creation of this book.

Library of Congress Cataloging-in-Publication Data

Halfmann, Janet.
Pelican's catch / by Janet Halfmann ; illustrated by Bob Dacey and Debra Bandelin.—1st ed.
p. cm.
Summary: Brown Pelican, who lives on a mangrove island off the coast of Puerto Rico, learns
how to fish and take care of herself. Includes facts about brown pelicans.
ISBN 1-59249-287-8 (hardcover)—ISBN 1-59249-286-X (micro hbk)—ISBN 1-59249-285-1 (pbk.)
  1. Brown pelican—Juvenile fiction. [1. Brown pelican—Fiction. 2. Pelicans—Fiction.]
  I. Dacey, Bob, ill. II. Bandelin, Debra, ill. III. Title.

PZ10.3
[E]—dc22

2004002577

PELICAN'S CATCH

by Janet Halfmann   Illustrated by Bob Dacey & Debra Bandelin

Where Children Discover...

As dawn lights up a small island of red mangrove trees off the southwest coast of Puerto Rico, a young brown pelican stretches her large wings. All around her, pelicans are waking up.

Brown Pelican is eleven weeks old. She hatched from an egg her mother laid in a nest high in a mangrove tree in this bay. Her parents recently helped her learn to fly. Now she must learn to fish for herself.

She soon gets her first chance. As a flock of pelicans fly out over the shallow water near the mangroves, Brown Pelican falls in line with them. She moves her long, powerful wings in rhythm with theirs, slowly flapping and then gliding. Soaring gracefully, the birds search with their keen eyes for schools of fish swimming in the clear, blue water.

Suddenly, one after another, the pelicans brake their flight. They have spotted a school of herring. One by one, the birds dive headfirst into the warm sea.

Brown Pelican is the last to go. Tipping downward, she folds her wings and aims her long bill like a spear at the water. She dive-bombs down twenty feet. Crash! Splash! Air pockets under her skin cushion her dive.

As Brown Pelican hits the water, her bill opens. The pouch on the bottom of her bill balloons into a big fishnet. When her bill snaps shut, it traps gallons of water.

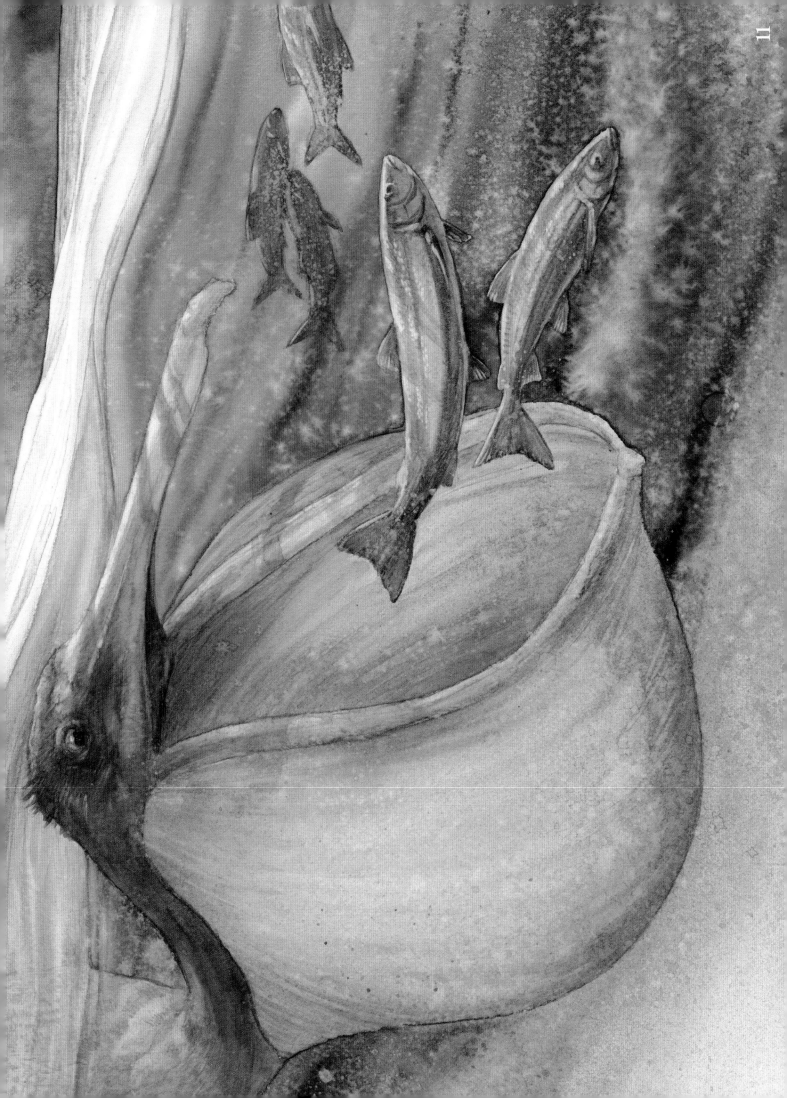

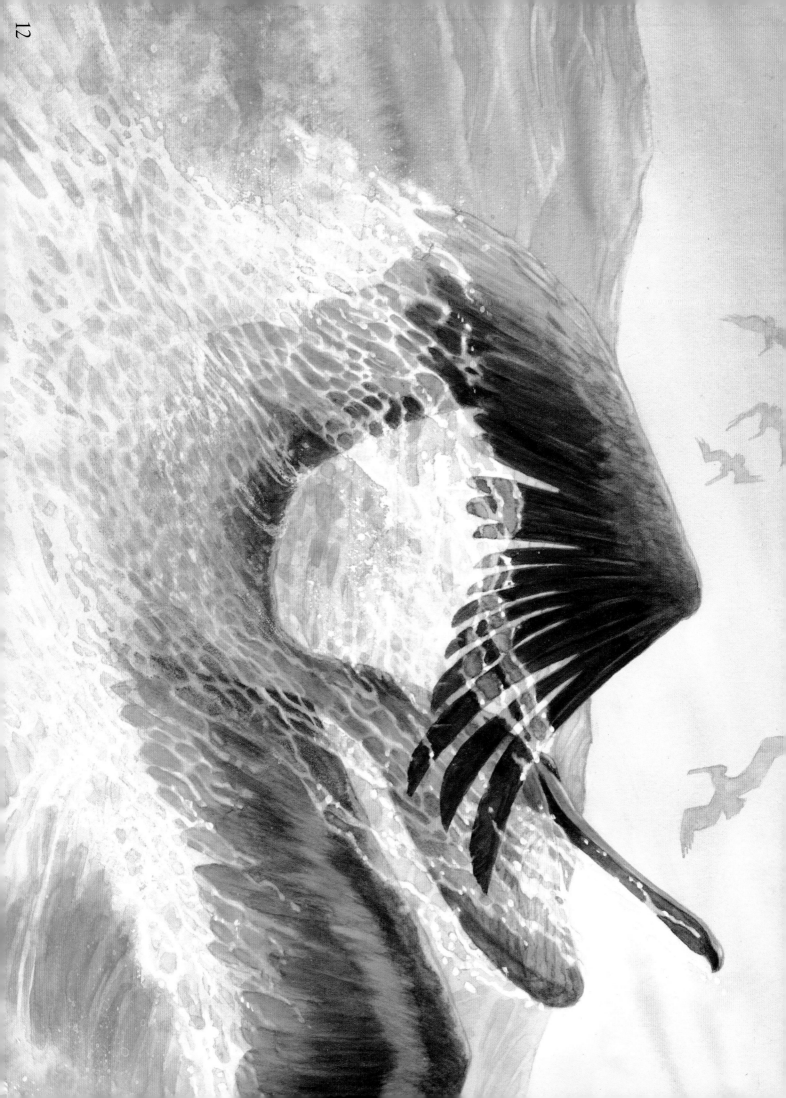

Now, Brown Pelican bobs to the surface like a cork. Gradually, she raises her head to let the water drain from her pouch. But where is the fish that she kept her eye on during her dive? Somehow, it escaped.

Brown Pelican wastes no time before she tries again. She faces into the wind, flaps her wings and churns her big webbed feet against the water. Soon she is in the air and soaring above the water once more.

For a long time, she soars and dives, soars and dives. Sometimes she traps a few fish in her pouch, but they always manage to wriggle free before she can swallow them!

Even though Brown Pelican's stomach is still empty, she is too tired to fish any longer without a rest. She follows a flock of pelicans to the mangroves edging the coastline.

Before Brown Pelican can rest, she needs a bath.
Her feathers are a mess after a morning of fishing.
First, she dips her bill in the warm water near the
mangroves. Then she thrashes her wings against
the surface, splashing water all over herself.

She flies up onto a twisted branch of the mangrove to preen. With her bill, she cleans and straightens each feather, then rubs them with oil from a gland near her tail. The oil makes her feathers waterproof, like a raincoat, so she will float.

Brown Pelican finds a shady spot in the mangroves and falls asleep. Late in the afternoon, the sounds of flapping wings wake her. She joins a flock of pelicans flying over the sea toward a lighthouse to fish until dusk.

In a small bay near the lighthouse, Brown Pelican spots a school of sardines and dives. She's in luck. Her pouch traps a fish. She bobs up. But a hungry gull immediately lands on her head.

What does the gull want? Brown Pelican quickly finds out. While she drains the water from her pouch, the gull grabs her sardine!

Up into the sky Brown Pelican soars again. She spots more fish, and down she dives. When she bobs up with her catch, the gull lands on her head again. But this time, Brown Pelican is ready. She quickly tosses her head back and swallows the fish before the gull can snatch it.

Brown Pelican fishes until the setting sun paints the sky red and orange. Her stomach is nearly full as she flies back to the mangrove island for the night. She sleeps well in her safe roost high above the sea.

With each new day, Brown Pelican will become better at fishing. With a bit of luck, she could be skydiving into the sea near the mangroves for another twenty or thirty years.

About the Brown Pelican

Pelicans are among the world's largest birds. The brown pelican, with a wingspan of 6.5 feet and a weight of 8 pounds, is the smallest of the family. Pelicans are best known for their enormous pouched bills. There are seven species of pelicans living near warm waters around the world. The brown pelican is very different from the rest. Most kinds of pelicans have primarily white feathers, live near inland lakes, and scoop up fish while swimming on the water. The brown pelican is mostly brown, lives near the sea and dives headfirst from the air for fish.

Brown pelicans live along coasts from central North America to northern South America. The brown pelican of this story, *Pelecanus occidentalis*, is one of six subspecies. It is the smallest of the brown pelicans, and adults have darker underparts. These pelicans live throughout the Caribbean region.

The Caribbean brown pelican is endangered. Its greatest threat is an unpredictable food supply. Food alternates between being abundant and scarce. Not so long ago, brown pelicans almost disappeared from North America. They recovered in many areas after the pesticide DDT was banned in the United States in 1972. DDT in the pelicans' food caused the birds to lay eggs with thin shells that cracked before the chicks could hatch. Today, there are about 105,000 breeding pairs of brown pelicans, including about 5,000 pairs of Caribbean brown pelicans.

Pelicans nest in colonies, usually on small islands. They build their nests of sticks, grass, and leaves in trees or on the ground. Female pelicans lay three eggs, but usually only one or two of the babies grow up. Parents feed their babies partly digested fish. Pelicans aren't completely grown up until they are three to five years old.

Glossary

Caribbean: The region of tropical islands between North and South America.

herring: Small saltwater fish in the sardine family.

mangrove trees: Trees with many tangled roots that grow at the edge of warm seas.

preen: To use the bill to clean, straighten, and waterproof feathers.

sardines: Small fish that live in salt water.

schools of fish: Large groups of fish swimming together.

waterlogged: Soaked or filled up with water.

webbed feet: Feet with pieces of skin joining the toes.

Points of Interest in this Book

pp. 4-5: mangrove trees.
pp. 10-11: school of fish.
pp. 22-23: lighthouse.
pp. 24-25: seagull.

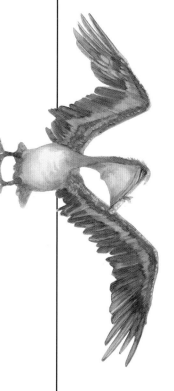